DUGGEE AND THE DINOSAURS

NORRIE   TAG   HAPPY   BETTY   DUGGEE   ROLY

Duggee is busy fixing his bicycle when
the Squirrels rush into the clubhouse.
"DUGGEE!" they shout. "What's this?"
Roly is holding a rock with a
squiggly bit on it.
It's a fossil!

THIS BOOK BELONGS TO

....

....

HEY DUGGEE

LADYBIRD BOOKS

UK | USA | Canada | Ireland | Australia | India | New Zealand | South Africa

Ladybird Books is part of the Penguin Random House group of companies whose addresses can be found at global.penguinrandomhouse.com.

www.penguin.co.uk   www.puffin.co.uk   www.ladybird.co.uk

 Penguin
Random House
UK

First published 2021
001

Text and illustrations copyright © Studio AKA Limited, 2021
Adapted by Rebecca Gerlings

Printed in China

The authorized representative in the EEA is Penguin Random House Ireland, Morrison Chambers, 32 Nassau Street, Dublin D02 YH68

A CIP catalogue record for this book is available from the British Library

ISBN: 978-1-405-94863-0

All correspondence to:
Ladybird Books
Penguin Random House Children's
One Embassy Gardens, 8 Viaduct Gardens, London SW11 7BW

FSC
www.fsc.org

MIX
Paper from
responsible sources
FSC® C018179

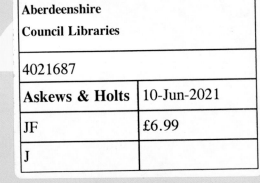

"What's a fossil?" asks Roly.
That's a BIG question, but Duggee can explain.
He has his **Fossil Badge!**

Fossils were made a long time ago, when the first creatures lived on Earth. Sometimes, incredible things happened, like . . .

BLIZZARDS!

VOLCANOES!

AND GREAT SANDSTORMS!

The creatures were then stuck for millions of years!

"Oooh!" gasp the Squirrels.
"Are there any more fossils?" asks Norrie.
"Ah-woof!" replies Duggee.
There are fossils of all sorts of creatures that lived millions of years ago.

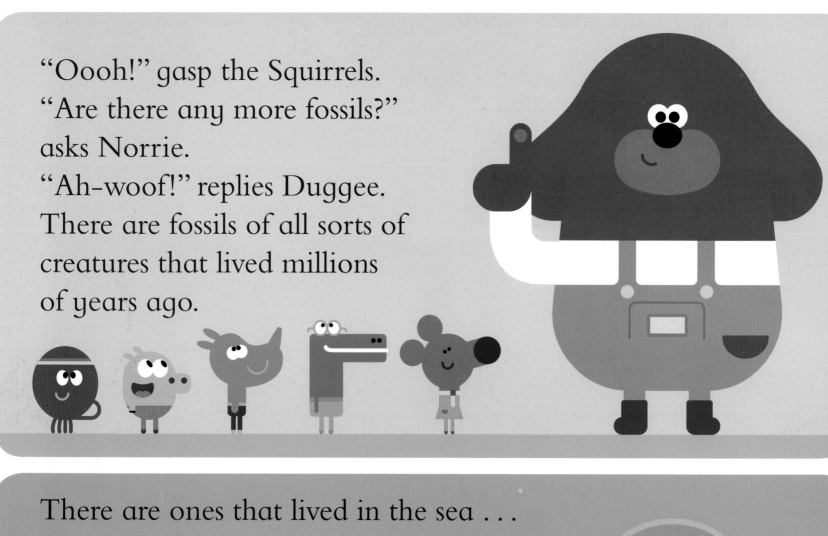

There are ones that lived in the sea . . .

ones that crawled out of the sea ...

small ones that flew and big ones that walked.
And they came in all shapes and sizes!

STOMP!

STOMP!

"Dinosaurs!" cries Betty excitedly.
"Like the **BETTY-SAURUS!**"

"TYRANNOS-ROLY REX!" roars Roly.

A TRI-TAG-ATOPS!

"A HAPPY-GATOR!" cries Happy.

SPLASHY! SPLASH!

When the dinosaurs left, the cavemen – or cave-Squirrels –
arrived, along with . . .
"Enid?" asks Tag.
No, that's a sabre-toothed tiger!

ROOOAR!

"Ethel?" asks Happy.
No, that's a woolly mammoth!

PARP-PARP-PARP!

"They look a bit like Enid and Ethel," says Norrie.
"But they look a bit different too."
Norrie's right – lots of things were different back then.

Roly runs into a cave to find some food. He runs
straight back out again, looking confused.
"Where's the kitchen?" he shouts.
There doesn't seem to be one.
"But how do we cook things?" exclaims Betty.

AH-WOOF!

Duggee makes a fire.
"Duggee's made a cooker!" says Tag.
That gives the Squirrels an idea.
"LET'S MAKE MORE STUFF!"
they shout.
Then they run off to get started.

Roly and Tag make a table and a chair from rock.

Betty and Norrie use a twig to make . . .
"A fork!" they cry.
And Happy uses a big leaf to make . . .
"A plate!" he cries.

But cave-Squirrels didn't stop there. They made
more stuff like . . .
"Art!" cries Norrie, dabbing paint on the cave wall.
And . . .

"Wheels!" shouts Tag, racing down a hill.

In fact, cave-Squirrels kept making new things . . .

CLATTER!

CLATTER!

. . . right up to now!

"So, from our tiny fossil, came *all* of this?" asks Norrie.

"Wow!" gasp the Squirrels.
"Fossils are AMAZING!" says Roly, gazing at the squiggly rock.

Haven't the Squirrels done well today, Duggee?
They have definitely earned their **Fossil Badges**.

Now there's just time for one more
thing before the Squirrels go home . . .